Cosmic Starlight Odyssey

Cosmic Starlight Odyssey

Odyssey, Volume 1

Anthony Fontenot

Published by Anthony Fontenot, 2024.

By Anthony Fontenot

© Anthony Fontenot

This is a work of fiction. Similarities to real people, places, or events are entirely coincidental.

Cosmic Starlight Odyssey

First edition. September 19, 2024.

Copyright © 2024 Anthony Fontenot

ISBN: 9798227163578

Written by Anthony Fontenot

This is a work of fiction. Similarities to real people, places, or events are entirely coincidental.

COSMIC STARLIGHT ODYSSEY

First edition. November 3, 2024.

Copyright © 2024 Anthony Fontenot.

ISBN: 979-8227163578

Written by Anthony Fontenot.

Table of Contents

Cosmic Starlight Odyssey 1
Chapter 1: The Cosmic Horizon 5
Chapter 2: The Web of Deceit 6
Chapter 3: The Heart of the Stronghold 8
Chapter 4: The Shadow Syndicate 12
Chapter 5: The Lost Operative 15
Chapter 6: Hidden Agenda 17
Chapter 7: The Device 18
Chapter 8: Nova's Agenda 20
Chapter 9: Aftermath 23
Chapter 10: Unleashed 26
Chapter 11: Nova's Revelation 29
Chapter 12: Cosmic Fade 31
Chapter 13: Galactic Rebirth 35
Chapter 14: Gateway to the Unknown 38
Chapter 15: Cosmic Origins 39
Chapter 16: Balance of the Cosmos 41
Chapter 17: Hidden Motives 46
Chapter 18: New Horizons 48
Chapter 19: Celestial Odyssey 50
Chapter 20: Legacy Unveiled 51
Chapter 21: The Quantum Leap 52

With heartfelt gratitude, thank you for being a shining light in my life. Your love and support mean everything.

"To my father, whose unwavering guidance and unconditional love have shaped me into the person I am today, thank you for being my rock and inspiration.

To Beth, whose kindness, compassion, and generosity have touched my life in countless ways, I honor and celebrate the impact you've made.

This Book is dedicated to you and with deepest gratitude and love.

"Thank you"

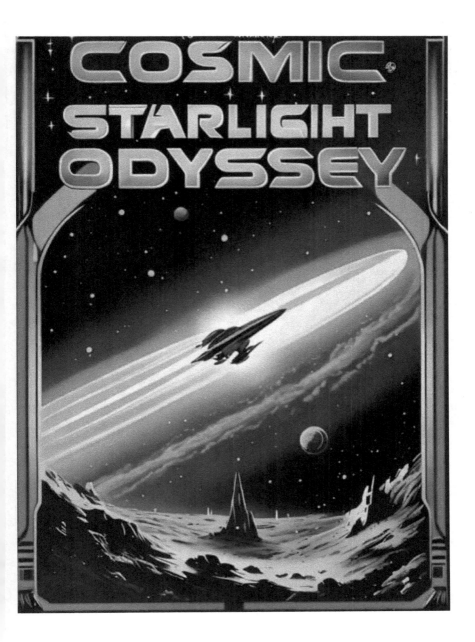

A cosmic Horizon

Chapter 1: The Cosmic Horizon

Humanity stood at the threshold of a new era, venturing deeper into the cosmos. Stars and galaxies beckoned, promising secrets and mysteries beyond imagination. But amidst the wonder, a threat lurked – the spread of
Fabricated stories and hoaxes threatened to undermine humanity's understanding of the universe. Powerful interests exploited the chaos, spreading false information through sophisticated algorithms. Public opinion was manipulated, and trust began to erode.
In response, the Cosmic Truth Initiative emerged, a coalition of intergalactic organizations united in their quest for fact-based information. Their mission was clear: promote critical thinking, develop cutting-edge misinformation detection tools, and foster a culture of transparency.
The forces of misinformation would not go quietly into the night. Agents of disinformation launched counterattacks, seeking to discredit the Cosmic Truth Initiative. But the advocates of truth stood firm, deploying AI-driven fact-checking bots and whistleblower protection programs. The battle for cosmic integrity had begun.

Chapter 2: The Web of Deceit

Agent Rachel Kim's eyes narrowed as she scrutinized Julian Saint Clair's every word. His revelation about the Echo Protocol had raised more questions than answers.
"What makes you think the Syndicate is after the Echo Protocol?" Rachel asked, her tone measured.
Julian leaned back, steepling his fingers. "I've seen classified documents. The Syndicate believes the Echo Protocol can amplify their control over cosmic frequencies, manipulating the fabric of space-time itself."
Rachel's mind raced. "And what's your role in this?"
Julian's gaze turned enigmatic. "Let's just say I have... motivations. Help me stop the Syndicate, and I'll ensure you get the truth."
Rachel hesitated, weighing the risks. Could she trust Julian?
Suddenly, her comms device beeped. "Agent Kim, we've detected unusual energy signatures near the Syndicate's HQ."
Rachel's instincts kicked in. "Looks like our move. Julian, you're coming with me."

As they approached the Syndicate's HQ, Rachel could feel the air thickening with tension. Julian's presence by her side was both reassuring and unsettling.

Upon arrival, they discovered a hidden entrance, guarded by elite agents.

"Julian, recognize anyone?" Rachel whispered.

Julian's eyes locked onto a familiar face. "That's Victor LaGrange. My... acquaintance."

Victor's gaze snapped toward Julian, his expression a mix of surprise and hostility.

"Julian Saint Clair. I didn't think you'd dare show your face here."

Rachel's grip on her blaster tightened. "This isn't a reunion. We're here for the Echo Protocol."

Victor sneered. "You're too late. The Protocol is already activated."

Rachel's eyes locked onto Victor. "What do you mean the Echo Protocol is activated?"

Victor's smile grew wider. "The Syndicate has harnessed its power. Cosmic frequencies are now under our control."

Julian's face darkened. "You fool, Victor. You don't understand the consequences."

Victor shrugged. "Consequences are for the weak. We'll reshape the cosmos in our image."

Rachel knew time was running out. "We need to shut down the Protocol."

Julian nodded. "I can guide you through the facility, but we'll face heavy resistance."

As they infiltrated the stronghold, blaster fire erupted around them. Syndicate agents closed in.

Chapter 3: The Heart of the Stronghold

Navigating through the labyrinthine corridors, Julian led Rachel to the Protocol's core.
"The Echo Protocol's energy signature is destabilizing the cosmos," Julian warned.
Rachel's determination hardened. "We'll stop this, no matter the cost."
Inside the core, they found the source of the energy signature: a massive crystal pulsating with cosmic energy.
Victor appeared, flanked by elite agents. "You'll never leave this place alive."
Rachel and Julian exchanged a glance. This was their last stand.
Rachel and Julian fought for survival, surrounded by Victor's elite agents.
"We need to disable the Protocol!" Rachel shouted.
"I'll try to hack the crystal's frequency!" Julian yelled back, returning fire.
The agents closed in, their blasters unleashing a hail of deadly bolts.
"We're outnumbered!" Rachel warned.
"Hold on!" Julian replied. "Almost there!"
Just as all seemed lost, the facility's alarms blared. The lights flickered.
"What's happening?" Rachel yelled.
"The Protocol's collapsing!" Julian shouted. "We have to get out!"
The room shook as the crystal's energy surged. Agents stumbled, disoriented.
"Now's our chance! Move!" Rachel ordered.
Together, they fought their way through the chaos.
Victor, enraged, lunged at Rachel. "You'll pay for this!"

Julian intervened, taking down the Syndicate leader. "Not today, Victor."
As they escaped the crumbling facility, Rachel turned to Julian. "We did it. The Protocol's down."
Julian's gaze lingered on the destruction. "This isn't over. The Syndicate will regroup."
Rachel's determination hardened. "We'll be ready. What's next?"
Julian's eyes locked onto hers. "Meet me on planet Nixxar. We have unfinished business."
Rachel's comms device beeped. "Agent Kim, report to HQ. Debriefing awaits."
"Understood," Rachel replied.
Julian's message followed: "Nixxar, Rachel. Don't forget."
Rachel's thoughts swirled with questions.
"Julian, what's on Nixxar?" she asked.
"Answers," Julian replied. "And more questions."
Rachel's agency director, Commander Patel, greeted her at HQ.
"Agent Kim, congrats on stopping the Protocol. But we have concerns."
"What kind?" Rachel asked.
"Rumors of a rogue agent within our ranks," Patel revealed. "And whispers of a hidden Syndicate faction."
Rachel's eyes narrowed. "I'll investigate."
Patel nodded. "Be careful, Agent Kim. The stakes are higher than ever."
Rachel's investigation into the rogue agent led her to a secluded sector of the agency's database. She uncovered a cryptic message:
"Project Elysium: Eyes only. Authorized personnel."
Rachel's curiosity piqued, she accessed the file.
"Project Elysium" revealed a shocking truth: the agency had secretly collaborated with the Syndicate to develop the Echo Protocol.
Rachel's stomach churned. "Who authorized this?"
A name caught her eye: Agent Thompson, her trusted colleague.
Rachel's comms device beeped. "Agent Kim, meet me on Nixxar."
Julian's message.

"Julian, I've found something," Rachel replied. "Project Elysium. Our agency's involved."
Julian's response was immediate. "I knew it. Meet me ASAP."
Rachel arrived on Nixxar, her mind reeling with questions.
Julian greeted her, his expression grim. "Rachel, we have a mole."
"Agent Thompson," Rachel revealed.
Julian nodded. "I suspected as much. Thompson's been feeding intel to the Syndicate."
Rachel's anger flared. "We need to bring them down."
Julian handed her a data pad. "Evidence is here. But we need more."
Their mission clear, they set out to gather proof and take down the rogue agents.
As they navigated the complex web of deceit, Rachel and Julian encountered unexpected allies and foes.
"Who can we trust?" Rachel asked.
Julian's gaze locked onto hers. "Each other. That's all we have."
Their bond strengthened, they forged ahead, determined to expose the truth.
But the Syndicate wouldn't go down without a fight.
Agent Thompson's betrayal cut deep. Rachel struggled to reconcile the colleague she thought she knew with the traitor before her.
"Why, Thompson?" Rachel demanded.
Thompson sneered. "The Syndicate promised power, resources... a new order."
Julian's eyes narrowed. "And what about our agency's director, Commander Patel?"
Thompson's smile grew wider. "Patel's been playing both sides. Syndicate loyalist, agency director... the perfect mole."
Rachel's world crumbled. Her trusted leader, a traitor?
Julian's grip on her arm steadied her. "We'll take them down, together."
Their mission clear, they infiltrated the agency's high-security facility.
Confronting Commander Patel, Rachel's emotions simmered.

"Sir, we have evidence," Rachel stated, her voice firm.
Patel's expression remained calm. "Evidence of what, Agent Kim?"
"Your ties to the Syndicate," Julian accused.
Patel's facade crumbled. "You're too late. The Syndicate's already in control."
Rachel's anger boiled over. "Not while I'm still breathing."
In a tense standoff, Rachel and Julian apprehended Patel.
As they escorted the director away, Rachel vowed, "Justice will be served."
But the Syndicate's grip remained strong.

Chapter 4: The Shadow Syndicate

In the shadows, Victor's successor, the enigmatic Archon, orchestrated the Syndicate's resurgence.
"Patel's fall is merely a setback," Archon declared. "Our true plan unfolds."
A mysterious figure emerged from the darkness.
"And what of Rachel Kim and Julian Saint Clair?" the figure asked.
Archon's smile sent chills down the figure's spine. "They'll soon learn the true meaning of power."
The stakes escalated. Rachel and Julian faced a revitalized enemy.
Archon's plan unfolded like a sinister tapestry. Rachel and Julian, now hunted by the Syndicate, fled to the underworld of Nixxar's shadowy districts.
"We need allies," Julian urged. "The Syndicate's too powerful."
Rachel nodded. "I know someone. Meet me at Club Erebus."
In the dimly lit club, they found Rachel's contact, the enigmatic smuggler, Phoenix.
"Phoenix, we need your help," Rachel requested.
Phoenix's gaze lingered on Julian. "What's in it for me?"

Julian smiled. "Access to Syndicate tech. Worth a fortune."
Phoenix nodded. "Deal. But I have conditions."
As they negotiated, Archon's agents closed in.
A traitor within Phoenix's ranks revealed their location. Syndicate forces stormed Club Erebus.
"Traitor!" Phoenix spat, executing the mole.
Rachel and Julian fought alongside Phoenix's crew, but they were outnumbered.
In the chaos, Julian disappeared.
"Julian!" Rachel screamed.
Phoenix grabbed her arm. "We must retreat. Now."
Rachel hesitated, then followed Phoenix.

Chapter 5: The Lost Operative

Rachel's search for Julian led her to the darkest corners of Nixxar.
"Julian, respond!" Rachel pleaded over comms.
Silence.
Days passed. Rachel's hope dwindled.
Then, a message:
"Meet me at sector 7. Come alone."
Julian's voice.
Rachel's heart skipped a beat.
Rachel arrived at sector 7, gun drawn.
Julian emerged from shadows, his eyes haunted.
"Rachel, I've been playing both sides," Julian confessed. "Syndicate and agency. I had to."
Rachel's world crumbled. "Why?"
Julian's gaze locked onto hers. "To protect you. The Syndicate wants you dead."
Rachel's trust wavered.
Rachel's eyes narrowed. "Why does the Syndicate want me dead, Julian?"
Julian hesitated. "Your past, Rachel. It's more complicated than you think."
Rachel's grip on her blaster tightened. "Tell me."
Julian's voice dropped to a whisper. "You were part of a secret program, codenamed 'Eclipse.' The Syndicate wants to exploit your unique skills."
Rachel's memories began to resurface.
"Eclipse... I remember fragments. Training, enhancements... and something went wrong."

Julian nodded. "The program was shut down, but the Syndicate revived it. They need your expertise for their plans."
Rachel's determination hardened. "I won't let them."
Archon addressed his inner circle. "Rachel Kim's Eclipse training makes her a valuable asset. Capture her, and we'll control the cosmos."
A hooded figure stepped forward. "I'll handle it."
The figure revealed: Agent Vega, Rachel's former Eclipse colleague.
"Vega, why?" Rachel asked, shocked.
Vega's gaze turned cold. "Loyalty, Rachel. To the Syndicate, and to ourselves."
The Eclipse program's dark secrets began to unravel.
Vega's revelation shook Rachel. "You're with the Syndicate?"
Vega's expression remained cold. "I adapted, Rachel. Eclipse trained us to survive."
Rachel's anger flared. "At what cost? Innocent lives?"
Vega shrugged. "Collateral damage. The Syndicate promises power, protection."
Rachel's determination hardened. "I won't join you, Vega."
Vega sneered. "You'll come willingly or by force."
Archon's voice echoed through the comms system. "Agent Vega, bring Rachel Kim alive."
Vega's team moved to surround Rachel.
Julian appeared, blaster blazing. "Not today, Vega."
Vega's eyes narrowed. "Julian Saint Clair. Traitor."
Julian fought alongside Rachel, taking down Vega's team.
As they escaped, Rachel confronted Julian. "Why did you help me?"
Julian's gaze locked onto hers. "Loyalty, Rachel. To you, not the Syndicate."
Rachel's trust wavered, but she saw sincerity in Julian's eyes.

Chapter 6: Hidden Agenda

In a secure hideout, Phoenix awaited them.

"Phoenix, what's your stake in this?" Rachel asked.

Phoenix leaned in. "Archon's plan threatens my operations. I want him taken down."

Julian's eyes narrowed. "What's Archon's plan?"

Phoenix hesitated. "Ancient technology... hidden on planet Arkeia."

Rachel's instincts flared. "What technology?"

Phoenix's voice dropped to a whisper. "A device capable of controlling the cosmos."

The stakes escalated.

Rachel's eyes widened. "A device controlling the cosmos? That's impossible."

Phoenix nodded. "Archon believes it's key to the Syndicate's dominance."

Julian's gaze turned calculating. "We need to get to Arkeia first."

Phoenix handed them a data pad. "Coordinates and intel. Be careful."

Rachel's determination hardened. "We won't let Archon control the cosmos."

On Arkeia, they navigated treacherous landscapes and ancient ruins.

Julian scanned their surroundings. "Energy signatures ahead."

Rachel drew her blaster. "Let's move."

Inside the ancient temple, they discovered cryptic artifacts and murals.

Vega's voice echoed through comms. "Rachel, surrender. Archon's patience wears thin."

Rachel's response was firm. "Never."

Chapter 7: The Device

Deep within the temple, they found the device: an orb pulsing with cosmic energy.

Julian's eyes locked onto the orb. "This is it. The key to controlling the cosmos."

Rachel's grip on her blaster tightened. "We can't let Archon have it."

Suddenly, the temple shook. Archon's forces breached the temple.

"Take the orb!" Archon ordered.

Vega and her team closed in.

Rachel aimed her blaster, firing at Vega's team. "Cover Julian!"

Julian sprinted toward the orb, dodging blaster fire.

Vega sneered. "You'll never escape!"

Rachel returned fire, taking down several agents.

Julian reached the orb, but Archon appeared, blaster pressed to Julian's head.

"Hand it over, Julian," Archon demanded.

Rachel's heart sank.

With a fierce cry, Rachel launched herself at Archon.

Blaster fire erupted around them.

Julian seized the distraction, tossing the orb to Rachel.

She caught it, feeling its energy course through her.

Archon's eyes widened. "No!"

Rachel fired her blaster point-blank at Archon.

The Syndicate leader stumbled back, wounded.

Vega's team retreated.

As the dust settled, Rachel helped Julian up.

"Thanks for the save," Julian said.

Rachel smiled grimly. "We're even."

The orb pulsed brighter, responding to Rachel's touch.

"What does it do?" Julian asked.

Rachel's eyes locked onto the orb. "I think it's connected to my Eclipse enhancements."

Suddenly, the temple began to destabilize.

"We need to get out – now!" Julian warned.

As they escaped the crumbling temple, Rachel pondered the orb's secrets.

"What's Phoenix's true motive?" Rachel asked.

Julian's gaze turned calculating. "Phoenix has ties to an ancient organization, hidden for centuries."

Rachel's eyes widened. "What organization?"

"The Order of the Nova," Julian revealed. "They seek balance in the cosmos."

Phoenix's voice echoed through comms. "Well done, Rachel. The orb's safe."

Rachel's distrust flared. "What's your stake in this, Phoenix?"

Phoenix hesitated. "I'm an Order agent. My mission: protect the orb from those who'd misuse its power."

Chapter 8: Nova's Agenda

At the Order's hidden base, Phoenix introduced Rachel and Julian to Nova's leader, Astrid.

Astrid's eyes shone with determination. "The orb's power can bring harmony or chaos. We must ensure its safekeeping."

Rachel's grip on the orb tightened. "I won't let it fall into Syndicate hands."

Astrid nodded. "We'll help you master the orb's energy."

Julian's gaze lingered on Astrid. "What's the true cost of Nova's protection?"

Astrid's expression turned enigmatic. "Alliances come with sacrifices, Julian."

Under Astrid's guidance, Rachel honed her skills, mastering the orb's energy.

"The orb responds to your Eclipse enhancements," Astrid explained.

Rachel's connection to the orb deepened, unlocking new abilities.

Julian observed, his expression thoughtful. "You're becoming a formidable force, Rachel."

Archon, wounded but determined, rallied the Syndicate.
"Capture Rachel Kim and the orb," Archon ordered. "Crush the Order of the Nova."
Vega led the assault on Nova's base.
Rachel, Julian, and Nova agents defended their stronghold.
The battle raged on.
As Syndicate forces breached the base, Rachel unleashed the orb's full power.
A blinding energy wave repelled the attackers.
Vega stumbled back, her eyes wide. "Impossible!"
Rachel stood firm, the orb's energy coursing through her.

"We won't be intimidated," Rachel declared.

Archon's voice echoed through comms. "You may have won this battle, but the war is far from over." The stakes escalated.

Chapter 9: Aftermath

The battle won, Rachel and Julian assessed the damage.
"Astrid, how bad is it?" Rachel asked.
Astrid's expression was grim. "We lost several agents. Our base is compromised."
Julian nodded. "We need to relocate, regroup."
Rachel's determination hardened. "We won't back down."
Nova's agents relocated to a secure facility.
Rachel began training with the orb, mastering its energy.
Julian worked with Nova's tech experts, analyzing Syndicate intel.
Astrid briefed them on Nova's next move.
"We have a lead on a Syndicate facility," Astrid said. "Intel suggests they're developing a countermeasure to the orb."
Rachel's eyes locked onto Astrid. "We need to infiltrate that facility."
Julian nodded. "I'll get to work on a plan."
Rachel, Julian, and a Nova team infiltrated the Syndicate facility.
They navigated through security systems and guards.
Rachel's orb-enhanced senses guided them.
Inside the lab, they discovered the countermeasure: a device capable of neutralizing the orb's energy.
Vega oversaw the project.
"Welcome, Rachel," Vega sneered. "You're just in time to witness the orb's downfall."
Rachel's grip on the orb tightened. "We can't let you neutralize its power."
Vega sneered. "You're too late. The countermeasure is online."
The device activated, emitting a frequency to disrupt the orb's energy.

Rachel felt the orb's power surging, resisting the countermeasure.
"No!" Vega shouted. "It can't—"
The orb released a blast of energy, overwhelming the device.
The countermeasure exploded, destroying the lab.
Vega stumbled back, shocked.
Rachel stood firm, the orb's energy coursing through her.

STARLIGHT ODYSSEY

Chapter 10: Unleashed

The orb's power spread, infiltrating the facility's systems.
Security systems failed. Alarms silenced.
Rachel, Julian, and the Nova team advanced, unopposed.
Archon's voice echoed through comms. "Vega, report!"
Vega's response was laced with fear. "The orb... it's out of control."
Archon's tone turned cold. "Contain it. At all costs."
The orb's energy continued to spread, disrupting the Syndicate's operations.
Rachel's connection to the orb deepened.
"I won't stop it," Rachel said, determination in her voice.
Julian's eyes locked onto hers. "What's the orb's plan?"
Rachel's gaze turned inward. "I'm not sure. But I trust it."
The orb's energy enveloped the facility, rewriting its infrastructure.
Systems merged, forming an interconnected network.
Rachel's consciousness expanded, becoming one with the orb.
She saw the cosmos, its secrets unfolding before her.
Julian's voice echoed, distant. "Rachel, what's happening?"
Rachel's response was barely audible. "I'm becoming... more."
The orb's power surged, propelling Rachel toward ascension.
Rachel's form began to shift, her molecular structure rearranging.
Her body glowed with an ethereal light, as if infused with stardust.
Julian's eyes widened. "Rachel, no! Don't lose yourself!"
Rachel's voice whispered in his mind. "I'm not losing myself, Julian. I'm finding my true self."
The orb's energy reached its zenith.
Rachel's transformation completed.

She stood tall, a being of cosmic energy.
Rachel's gaze swept the cosmos, perceiving hidden patterns.
Galaxies aligned, their secrets revealed.
The Syndicate's strongholds crumbled, their power broken.
Archon's voice trembled. "Impossible... She's become a—"
Julian finished the thought. "A cosmic entity."
Rachel's voice echoed through the cosmos. "I am the balance. The orb's power, now mine."
Rachel's presence resonated throughout the cosmos, restoring equilibrium.
Stars aligned, planets stabilized, and galaxies harmonized.
The Syndicate's remnants scattered, leaderless.
Archon's voice whispered, defeated. "It's over."
Julian approached Rachel, awe-struck.
"Rachel, you're... radiant."
Rachel's cosmic form smiled.
"I've become what I was meant to be."

Chapter 11: Nova's Revelation

Astrid appeared, her eyes shining.
"Rachel, you've fulfilled Nova's prophecy."
Rachel's gaze turned inward.
"What prophecy?"
Astrid's voice filled with reverence.
"You are the Celestial Key, unlocking balance in the cosmos."
Rachel's understanding deepened.
"I see. My journey, the orb, it was all leading to this."
Rachel's cosmic form expanded, encompassing the galaxy.
"I will maintain balance, protect the cosmos."
Julian stood beside her, steadfast.
"Together, we'll ensure peace."
Astrid nodded.
"Nova will support you, Rachel. Always."
The cosmos flourished under Rachel's guardianship.
Rachel convened the Celestial Council, gathering cosmic entities.
Ancient beings from distant galaxies attended.
Rachel's presence commanded respect.
"The cosmos needs unity," Rachel declared. "Together, we'll maintain balance."
The council agreed, acknowledging Rachel's leadership.
Under Rachel's guidance, galaxies flourished.
Civilizations prospered, exploring the cosmos.
Julian and Astrid worked alongside Rachel.
Nova's agents became cosmic ambassadors.
The Syndicate's remnants disbanded.

Rachel's legend grew, inspiring generations.
Stars were named after her.
Planets bore her likeness.
Rachel's cosmic form smiled.
"I've created a legacy of balance."
Julian's eyes shone.
"Your legacy will endure."
Astrid nodded.
"Nova's prophecy fulfilled."
Epilogue: Celestial Horizon
Rachel's cosmic form gazed into the horizon.
The cosmos stretched before her.
Endless possibilities awaited.
Rachel's voice whispered.
"I am the Celestial Key."
The galaxy Fade to black.

Chapter 12: Cosmic Fade

The galaxy's vibrant colors dulled.
Stars dimmed, their light extinguished.
Planets cooled, their atmospheres collapsing.
Rachel's cosmic form stood alone.
"The balance is shifting," Rachel whispered.
Julian's voice echoed, distant.
"Rachel, what's happening?"
Rachel's gaze swept the fading galaxy.
"Energy is draining... The cosmos is collapsing."
Astrid's voice trembled.
"Is this the end?"
The void, a vast emptiness, spread.
Galaxies disappeared, consumed.
Rachel's form began to fade.
"I must find the source," Rachel said.
Julian's determination flared.
"We'll find a way to stop this."
Astrid's eyes locked onto Rachel.
"Use the orb's power."
Rachel's cosmic form concentrated.
The orb's energy surged.
Rachel pierced the quantum threshold.
A hidden realm revealed itself.
Ancient entities, architects of the cosmos, awaited.
"You have reached the nexus," they said.
Rachel's determination hardened.

"I won't let the galaxy die."
The architects' response echoed.
"Balance requires sacrifice."
The architects revealed the cosmos' true nature.
"Balance requires renewal," they said.
Rachel's determination hardened.
"I won't let the galaxy die."
The architects presented a choice.
"Sacrifice your cosmic form, Rachel."
Julian's voice trembled.
"Rachel, no!"
Astrid's eyes locked onto Rachel.
"Trust the architects."
Rachel's resolve deepened.
"I'll save the galaxy."
Rachel surrendered her cosmic form.
Energy released, revitalizing the galaxy.
Stars rekindled, planets warmed.
Life burst forth, renewed.
The void receded, its darkness vanquished.
Julian's voice whispered.
"Rachel?"
Astrid's smile shone.
"She's become the galaxy itself."
Epilogue: Eternal Balance
The galaxy flourished, balanced.
Rachel's essence infused every star.
Julian and Astrid roamed the cosmos.
Their hearts carried Rachel's legacy.
The orb, now a beacon, guided civilizations.
In the distance, a whisper echoed.
"I am the galaxy."

Chapter 13: Galactic Rebirth

Rachel's whispered words echoed through the cosmos. "I am the Galaxy."
As her essence infused every molecule, stars pulsed and planets aligned. A new era dawned, and with it, a renewed sense of hope.
Rachel's consciousness expanded, unlocking secrets of the galaxy. Her transformation was complete – she had become one with the cosmos.
"Rachel?" Julian called out.
Astrid's eyes shone. "She's everywhere now."
Julian nodded. "Her legacy shines brighter than any star."
Under Rachel's guidance, civilizations flourished. Planets once barren now teemed with life. The orb, now a celestial compass, directed explorers to hidden wonders.
Julian and Astrid roamed the galaxy, sharing Rachel's wisdom. Together, they forged a new era of peace and cooperation.
"Cosmic balance has been restored," Astrid said.
Julian smiled. "Rachel's spirit ignites the cosmos."
Rachel's symphony echoed through the galaxy. Stars sang in harmony, planets danced. Galactic balance was perfected.
Astrid smiled. "Rachel's legacy will endure forever."
Julian nodded. "Her spirit is eternal."
An ancient prophecy unfolded. "A cosmic guardian will rise."
Rachel's essence stirred. "A new threat emerges."
The galaxy responded, preparing for battle. Julian and Astrid stood ready.
"What's coming?" Julian asked.
Rachel's voice whispered. "The unknown."

Julian and Astrid patrolled the galaxy, ever vigilant.
Rachel's essence guided them, sensing disturbances.
A faint signal echoed from a distant planet.
"Anomaly detected," Astrid said.
Julian's eyes narrowed. "Let's investigate."
They landed on the planet, surrounded by ancient ruins.
Rachel's essence stirred, unlocking secrets.
"An ancient civilization," Astrid whispered.
Julian's gaze swept the horizon. "And a hidden threat."
A structure rose, emitting energy.
"What is this?" Julian asked.
Rachel's voice whispered. "A gateway."

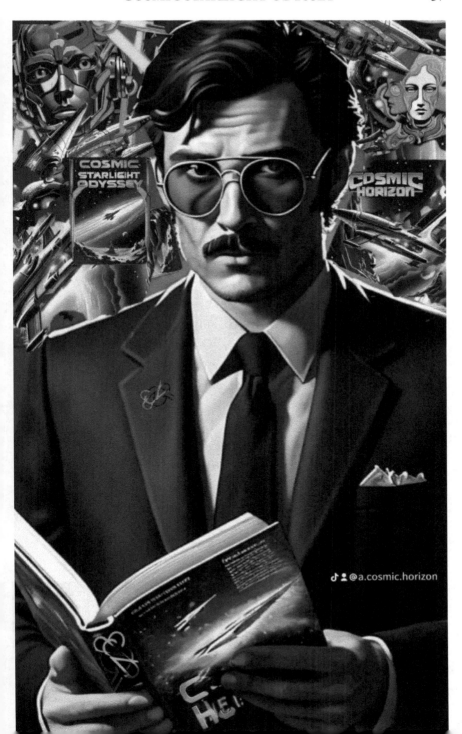

Chapter 14: Gateway to the Unknown

The gateway activated, revealing a wormhole.
Julian and Astrid exchanged a glance.
"Rachel, what lies beyond?" Julian asked.
Rachel's essence pulsed. "The unknown."
Julian and Astrid stepped into the wormhole.
Rachel's essence enveloped them, guiding their journey.
Stars blurred, space-time distorted.
They emerged in a realm beyond their galaxy.
Ancient structures towered, emitting mystical energy.
Julian's eyes widened. "This is impossible."
Astrid's voice filled with awe. "Rachel's legacy."
A figure approached, cloaked in shadows.
"Welcome, guardians," the figure said.
The figure revealed itself: an ancient being.
"I hold secrets of the cosmos," it said.
Rachel's essence stirred, curious.
"What secrets?" Julian asked.
The ancient being smiled. "The origin of the universe."

Chapter 15: Cosmic Origins

The ancient being's words echoed through Julian's mind. "The origin of the universe?" he repeated, his voice barely above a whisper.

Astrid's eyes sparkled with curiosity. "Tell us," she urged.

The ancient being nodded, its presence shimmering with an otherworldly energy. "In the beginning, there was the Void," it began. "An endless expanse of nothingness, punctuated by a single point of light."

Rachel's essence pulsed, as if resonating with the ancient being's words.

"That point of light expanded, birthing the universe," the being continued. "Matter coalesced, forming galaxies and stars. Life emerged, evolving into complex forms."

Julian's mind reeled, struggling to comprehend the sheer scale of creation.

"What about the Quantum Core?" Astrid asked, her voice filled with determination.

The ancient being's smile grew wider. "Ah, the Quantum Core. A key to unlocking the universe's secrets, hidden within the fabric of space-time."

Rachel's essence stirred, as if urging Julian and Astrid onward.

"Come," the ancient being said. "Witness the birth of the universe."

The ancient being led Julian and Astrid through a shimmering portal. They found themselves floating amidst swirling clouds of gas and dust. A brilliant light illuminated the cosmos. Stars burst forth, their radiance casting an ethereal glow.

Planets coalesced, their orbits weaving a celestial tapestry. Life sprouted, evolving from simple organisms to complex civilizations.

Rachel's essence resonated with the universe's symphony.

"This is incredible," Astrid whispered.

Julian's gaze swept the cosmic landscape. "We're witnessing the universe's birth."

The ancient being's voice whispered in their minds. "Remember, guardians. The Quantum Core holds the key to balancing the universe's energies."

Chapter 16: Balance of the Cosmos

As they returned to the ancient structure, Julian felt an overwhelming sense of purpose.
"What must we do?" Astrid asked, determination etched on her face.
Rachel's essence pulsed. "Restore balance to the Quantum Core."
The ancient being nodded. "The fate of the universe depends on it."
With newfound resolve, Julian and Astrid stepped forward, ready to face the challenges ahead.
Will they succeed in restoring balance to the Quantum Core?
Julian and Astrid stood before the ancient being, determination burning within them. "We won't fail," Julian vowed.
Astrid's eyes shone with conviction. "We'll restore balance to the Quantum Core."
The ancient being's smile held mystical depths. "The prophecy unfolds. Rachel's essence guides you."
Suddenly, visions flooded Julian's mind: swirling energies, quantum fluctuations and the Cosmic Horizon's secrets.

"The path ahead," the ancient being whispered, "is fraught with danger. Time and space converge."

Julian and Astrid stepped into the wormhole, Rachel's essence enveloping them. Stars blurred, space-time distorted.

They emerged near the NeuroSphere facility, now a hub of frantic activity.

Dr. Patel rushed toward them. "Julian, Astrid! We've stabilized the Quantum Core, but—"

"A temporal convergence is happening," Julian interrupted, visions still seared in his mind.

Astrid's grip on her weapon tightened. "We must protect the Core."

Forces converged on NeuroSphere: rival factions, ancient enemies and time-travelers.

Julian, Astrid and Dr. Patel's team defended the Quantum Core against those seeking to exploit its power.

Rachel's essence surged, amplifying Julian's abilities.

In the heart of the battle, an unexpected ally emerged.

As the battle raged on, Julian's thoughts drifted to his troubled past. His parents, renowned scientists, had disappeared during an experiment when he was a teenager. The incident left emotional scars.

Astrid's gaze met Julian's, her expression softening. "Hey, focus!" she shouted above the din.

Julian snapped back to reality, his determination renewed.

Astrid's Backstory

Astrid's thoughts wandered to her own past. Growing up on the streets, she had to rely on her wits and fists. Her natural talent for combat earned her a spot in an elite military unit.

But the memories of her fallen comrades continued to haunt her.

Dr. Patel's Secrets

Dr. Patel's eyes locked onto Julian, her expression a mix of concern and admiration. She recalled her own journey: a brilliant mind, driven by curiosity and a hidden agenda.

Her thoughts whispered: "The Quantum Core holds more than energy – it holds the key to unlocking humanity's true potential."

Rachel's Legacy

Rachel's essence pulsed, her presence woven into the fabric of the Quantum Core. Her memories unfolded: love, loss and sacrifice. "Julian," Rachel's voice whispered in his mind, "balance the Core, restore hope."

Chapter 17: Hidden Motives

As forces clashed, tensions escalated. Alliances were tested.
Dr. Patel approached Julian. "We need to recalibrate the Quantum Core. Trust me."
Astrid hesitated. "What's your true agenda, Doctor?"
Dr. Patel's smile hinted at secrets untold. "The future of humanity hangs in balance."
Julian's instincts screamed caution, but Rachel's essence reassured him.
"Trust her," Rachel whispered.
Julian nodded, trusting Rachel's guidance.

"Let's do it, Dr. Patel."

Astrid's eyes narrowed. "We're risking everything."
Dr. Patel's hands flew across the console. "We're altering the Quantum Core's resonance frequency."
The room hummed with tension as calculations streamed across screens.
The Quantum Core pulsed, its energy signature shifting.
Rachel's essence swirled, merging with the Core.
Astrid's grip on her weapon tightened. "What's happening?"
Dr. Patel's eyes sparkled. "Resonance achieved."
The Quantum Core's glow stabilized, its power now balanced.
Julian exhaled, relief washing over him.
Astrid's smile hinted at pride. "We did it."
Dr. Patel's expression turned contemplative. "This changes everything."

Chapter 18: New Horizons

The NeuroSphere facility transformed into a hub of discovery. Scientists flocked to unlock the Quantum Core's secrets. Julian, Astrid and Dr. Patel stood at the forefront.
Rachel's essence whispered, "The universe awaits."
A shimmering portal emerged from the Quantum Core.
Astrid's eyes widened. "A gateway to the cosmos."
Julian's heart raced. "Where does it lead?"
Dr. Patel's smile held wonder. "Let's find out."
Julian's hand reached out, hesitating before touching the shimmering portal. Astrid's gaze met his, excitement and trepidation mingling. Dr. Patel's voice filled the silence. "This gateway holds secrets of the universe. Let's uncover them."
With a deep breath, Julian stepped forward, Astrid beside him. The portal enveloped them, colors blurring as they traversed the vast expanse. Stars streaked past, like diamonds on velvet. Nebulae unfolded, ethereal curtains of gas and dust.

Chapter 19: Celestial Odyssey

They emerged on the edge of a nebula, its swirling clouds shimmering. Astrid's gasp echoed through the void. "Incredible." A celestial city floated within the nebula's heart, shimmering spires reaching toward the stars.

Julian's awe was palpable. "An ancient civilization." Dr. Patel's eyes sparkled. "One holding secrets of the cosmos."

The trio approached the city, guarded by beings of pure energy. Their forms shifted, like liquid light. "Welcome, travelers," one being said. "We have awaited you."

Rachel's essence stirred within Julian. "These guardians hold the universe's truths."

Within the city's heart, an ancient artifact pulsed. The guardians' leader spoke, "This artifact holds the universe's origins." Dr. Patel's hands reached out, reverence in her eyes.

As the artifact activated, visions flooded their minds: cosmic birth, celestial dance and the Quantum Core's secrets.

Chapter 20: Legacy Unveiled

The visions faded, leaving stunned silence. Astrid whispered, "The universe's secrets." Julian's gaze locked onto Dr. Patel. "What does this mean?"

Dr. Patel's smile was radiant. "We hold the key to unlocking humanity's potential."*Chapter

Dr. Patel's eyes shone with excitement. "The artifact revealed the universe's blueprint. We can harness this knowledge to elevate human consciousness."

Astrid leaned in, intrigued. "Explain, Doctor."

"The Quantum Core resonates with humanity's collective unconscious," Dr. Patel began. "By synchronizing our minds with its frequency, we can tap into limitless potential."

Julian's mind raced. "Telepathy, telekinesis?"

Dr. Patel nodded. "And more. Enhanced cognition, accelerated healing. Humanity's next evolution."

Chapter 21: The Quantum Leap

Rachel's essence pulsed, resonating with Dr. Patel's words.
"The Quantum Core's balance restored, we can initiate the quantum leap," Dr. Patel announced.
Astrid's determination hardened. "Let's do this."
Julian's resolve deepened. "Together, we'll unlock humanity's future."
NeuroSphere's team worked tirelessly, constructing a global network.
Dr. Patel oversaw the operation. "When activated, this network will synchronize human consciousness with the Quantum Core."
Astrid and Julian stood ready, their bond stronger than ever.
The network hummed to life. Energy surged, enveloping the planet. Humanity's collective unconscious stirred, awakening dormant potential.
*As the energy dissipated, silence fell.
The first thought echoed through minds worldwide:
"We are one."

COSMIC STARLIGHT ODYSSEY

A cosmic Horizon

Don't miss out!

Visit the website below and you can sign up to receive emails whenever Anthony Fontenot publishes a new book. There's no charge and no obligation.

https://books2read.com/r/B-A-STPNB-VARCF

BOOKS2READ

Connecting independent readers to independent writers.

Did you love *Cosmic Starlight Odyssey*? Then you should read *Cosmic horizon*[1] by Anthony Fontenot!

"The Quantum Core, a revolutionary device harnessing quantum energy, holds the key to solving humanity's energy crisis. But as Dr. Sofia Patel's team delves deeper, they discover a catastrophic rift in the quantum field, threatening to destroy reality. Can they tame the device's power before it's too late, or will their discovery be humanity's undoing?"Science Fiction fans
    Readers interested in technological thrillers
    Enthusiasts of speculative fiction and futuristic stories
    Read more at www.tiktok.com/@a.cosmic.horizon.

---

1. https://books2read.com/u/boonkZ

2. https://books2read.com/u/boonkZ

About the Author

A born and raised Texan, Anthony Fontenot will usually introduce himself as "basically Hank Hill". The casual observer may note that he has a very nice beard, unlike his animated counterpart. He collects VHS tapes, specifically of the horror and sci-fi genres. He's worked a myriad of jobs, his favorite being part of the team at Ripley's Believe It Or Not!, as well as being a light and sound technition for local and touring major music artists. He currently makes his living as a security guard. He enjoys making art, going to concerts, and spending time with family and friends.

Read more at www.tiktok.com/@a.cosmic.horizon.

Milton Keynes UK
Ingram Content Group UK Ltd.
UKHW022021131124
451149UK00013B/1237